Clown

QUENTIN BLAKE

HENRY HOLT AND COMPANY

NEW YORK

for Christine

Henry Holt and Company, LLC
Publishers since 1866
175 Fifth Avenue
New York, New York 10010
www.HenryHoltKids.com

First published in the United States in 1996 by Henry Holt and Company
Originally published in Great Britain in 1995 by Jonathan Cape,
a division of Random House UK Limited

Library of Congress Cataloging-in-Publication Data
Blake, Quentin. Clown / Blake.
Summary: After being discarded, Clown makes his way through town having a series of
adventures as he tries to find a home for himself and his other toy friends.
[1. Toys—Fiction.   2. Home—Fiction.   3. Stories without words.]   I. Title.
PZ7.B56Cl   1996   [E]—dc20   95-12811

ISBN-13: 978-0-8050-5933-5 / ISBN-10: 0-8050-5933-4
5   7   9   10   8   6

First American hardcover edition published in 1996 by Henry Holt and Company
First American paperback edition, 1998

Printed in Singapore

The artist used watercolor and ink to create the illustrations for this book.